DATE DUE

FEB 2 0 2016		

THE SCARY SHOW OF MO AND JO

THE SCARY SHOW
OF MO AND JO

by Hanoch Piven

RUNNING PRESS
KIDS
PHILADELPHIA·LONDON

To the "real" Mo, Jo, and O.

9 8 7 6 5 4 3 2 1
Digit on the right indicates the number of this printing

Library of Congress Control Number: 2005901832

ISBN 0-7624-2097-9

Cover and interior design by Frances J. Soo Ping Chow
Edited by Elizabeth Encarnacion
Typography: Abadi and Badhouse

This book may be ordered by mail from the publisher.
Please include $2.50 for postage and handling.
But try your bookstore first!

Published by Running Press Kids, an imprint of
Running Press Book Publishers
125 South Twenty-second Street
Philadelphia, Pennsylvania 19103-4399

Visit us on the web!
www.runningpress.com

This is Mo and this is Jo.

They are both quite sweet, although...

They'd love to scare you from head to toe!

"Let's put on a show," says Mo.

"A creepy, crawly, scary show!"

"THE SCARY SHOW OF MO AND JO!"

But how can they *really* scare?

They're both so sweet.

How can they play tricks instead of treats?

"I have a wonderful idea," says Mo.

"A witch is the most chilling thing I know!"

"So, let's see, what can I use
to give my brother Jo the blues?"

A witch needs a nose,

some hair of straw,

and stinky garlic teeth so raw!

Put it all together, and what do you get?

"I still need something before I'm through:
the right hat for making my witch's brew."

"Am I scary?"

The
WILDEST,
WICKEDEST
WITCH
you've met!

But Jo, he is no easy foe.

"I'll show Mo who is the pro."

A MAGNIFICENT
WIZARD
that will make Mo flee!

"As a wizard dressed in black,
I could go on the attack!"

A wizard needs a nose,

a long, stringy beard,

and some teeth that aren't too weird.

Put it all together and what do you see?

"I need a special hat for extra power.
This cone is perfect—it'll make Mo cower!"

"Now, am I scary?"

"Jo, you may have a great wizard's hat,
but with my magic I'll turn you into a..."

"Very funny, Mo, but I'm the master of this house. Watch how I turn you into a..."

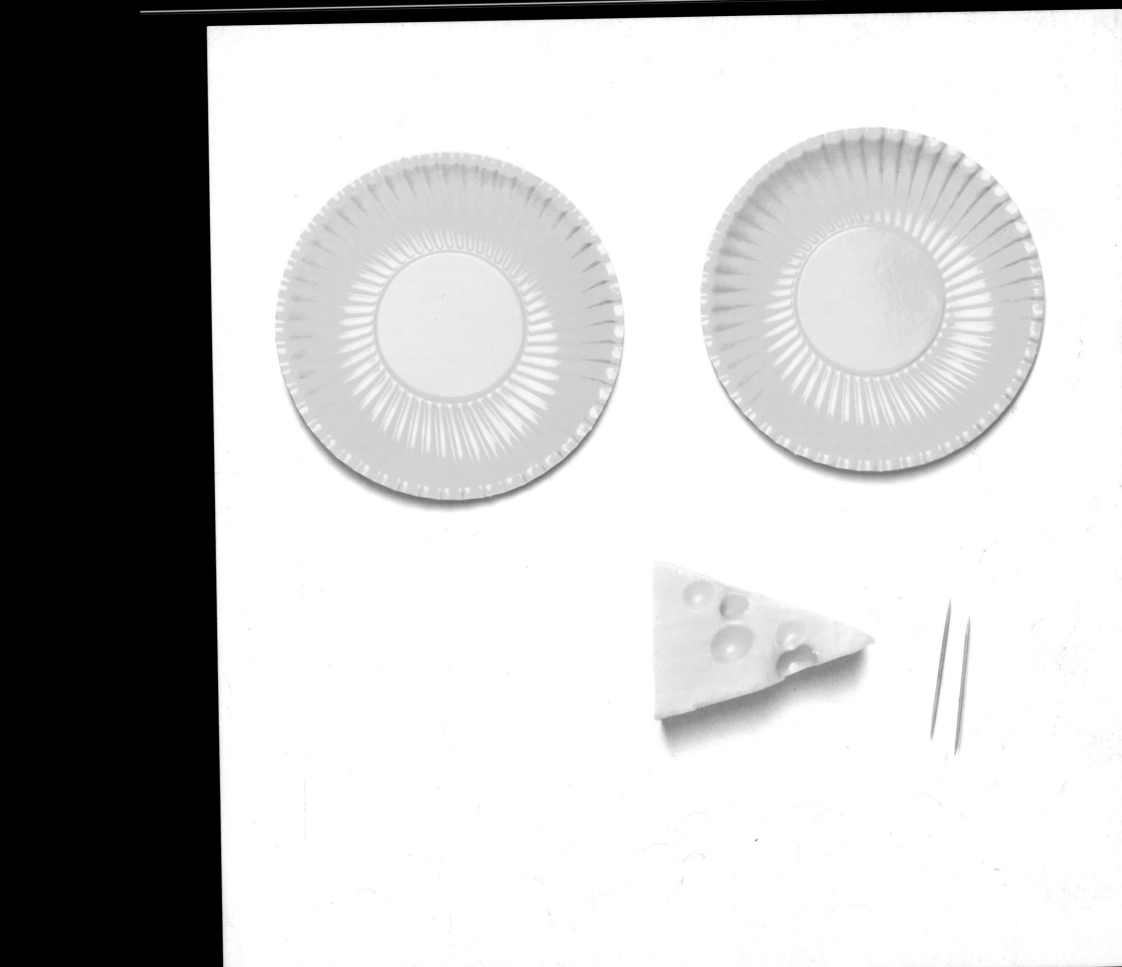

"MOUSE!"

"Now, what will I do with these—can you guess?
I will change myself into a..."

"ROARING LIONESS!"

"Kitty, Kitty."

"Show some pity."

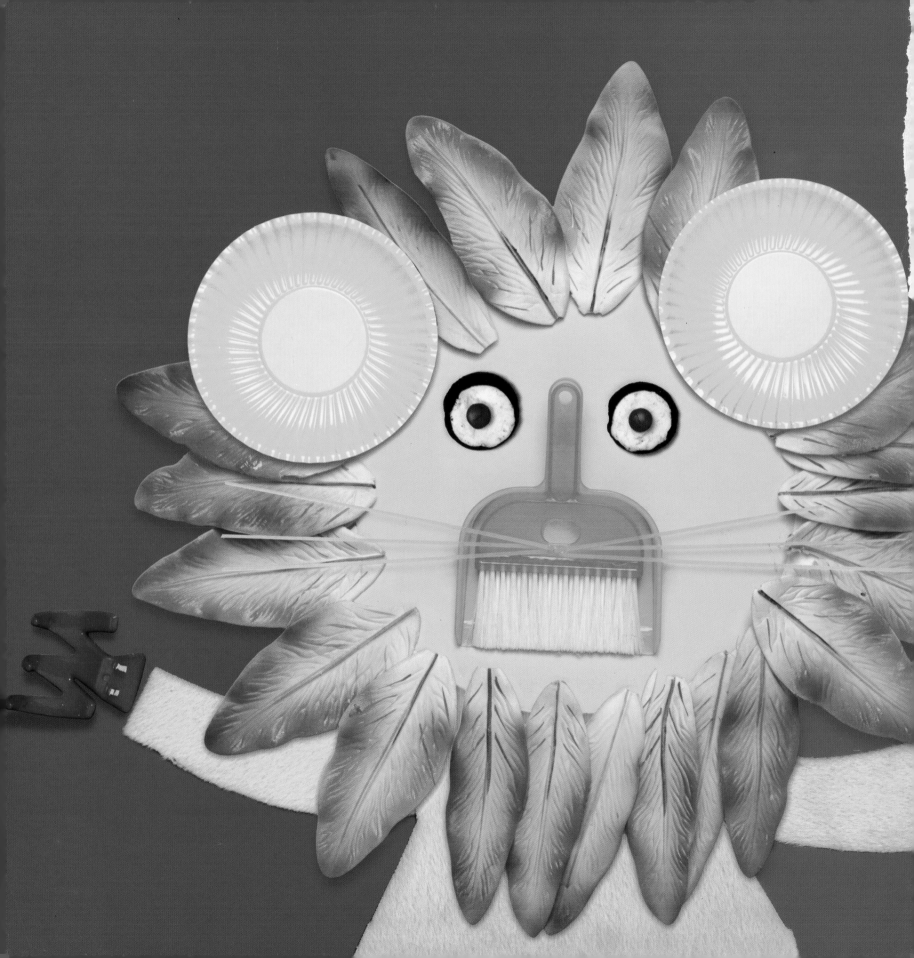

"Well, Mo, if that is your desire,
I'll become a..."

"DRAGON
breathing fire!"

Yes, Mo and Jo put on a great show,

But what is this
chilling sound below?

"BOoooOooo"

"RUN!"

shouts Mo.

"GO, GO, GO!"

screams Jo.

"Is that a tiger, a wolf, a crow?"

"A giant monster from long ago?"

"Is he trying to stop our show?"

NO, NO, NO.

It's just your baby brother, Bo.

"Ohhhhhhhhhh."

A Note from Hanoch Piven

I love drawing...with objects! Drawing is not only about making actual lines. It is about seeing, observing, and noticing.

If you take two buttons, a carrot, and a plastic bottle top and move them around on a cardboard circle cutout, you'll be drawing with objects, too. See how many different faces and facial expressions you can make just by moving these simple elements.

Now, what if you added more objects of different shapes, different colors, and different sizes? That is what this book is all about...

The Scary Show of Mo and Jo is a little workshop that shows how I choose which things to use in my "drawings," but you might think of a better way of testing and selecting the perfect ones. The important thing is to use your creativity to look at the things around you in a new way.

I hope this story will inspire you to do your own drawings with objects. Send them to me, if you'd like.

Love,
Hanoch
hanoch@pivenworld.com